# SHORTS:

## A Collection

JA Carter-Winward

Binary Press 2013

Published by Binary Press Publications, LLC

ISBN-13: 978-1-61171-022-9

ISBN-10: 1611710227

# Dedication

To Kent, my love.

# Contents

# Clinic

The car door closes behind the girl, and without stopping, she walks to the sidewalk. The girl wears a gray hoodie jacket, lined with flannel. It's not a parka, but it's warm enough against the chill. Her hands delve deep into her pockets and strain the coat away from her body. Her fists show through the cloth and extend forward as if they're trying to escape their owner. As she stands on the sidewalk, she slides her hands out of their cocoons. Slowly, her elbows rise behind her so she can rest the palms of her hands on her lower back. For a moment her shoulders collapse, curving her back into a "C" shape; her black ponytail flops forward against her cheek and she grimaces in discomfort as her protruding belly seems to disappear behind her jacket.

She straightens and looks back at the car expectantly.

A young man emerges from the driver's side and steps up to the curb. His feathery-thin mustache barely shadows his lip. Smoke balloons around his face like fogged glass as the tip of his cigarette brightens momentarily. Black eyes flit around the lot. Untouched by anything he sees, he turns to face the girl. They stare at each other and she, too, glances at her surroundings with a slight frown. The sun barely scrapes the tops of the mountains—the new morning rays have just emerged over the snow-capped peaks. She raises a delicate hand to her brow to ward off the rising light.

Her lips move and he nods his head in assent but his face registers nothing but a void mien. With a twist of her neck she flips her ponytail back in place. As she turns to face the blonde-brick strip

1

mall facade, her gait is unsteady. Her ample abdomen seems to reach forward and propel her toward the door.

The young man waits near the car as she reaches for the shiny gold knob of a door. She holds it open for a moment, her back to him. Eyes closed, he devours the smoke with collapsing cheeks, an intense draw that lights the end of the cigarette to a final blaze. With a furtive look around, he tosses the smoking butt to the sidewalk.

It seems to take him an eternity to reach the door. His feet shuffle with small steps, as when a young boy's feet sinks in sand on a beach. Unaware of his proximity, the girl lets the door close behind her. He stops and regards the closed door. He does not reach for the handle right away. Instead, he stops and surreptitiously glances about the sidewalk and parking lot once more. His face is passive, hollow and resigned. He reaches for the gold handle and walks through the door behind his companion. He enters the clinic, seemingly alone.

# Large Coffee

*...how could getting coffee be so fucking difficult? no, i shouldn't think like that. she's young and the line's long. jesus, what's the count now? eighteen. that's...yeah...eighteen hours. they told me i'd have days and nights that run into days but they never tell you how bright mornings are after. after shift, after ER lights burn fucking holes through your skull. shit. i slept like shit and i jumped for the phone every five minutes. never doing this again. they want me on-call, fine, but not before...*

His hand reaches out, a disembodied specter from his pocket. The white receipt blurs and the numbers run into letters into numbers as he signs his name and he tells the barista he'll wait outside. Her brown eyes glance at his: up, then down. He checks his forearms for blood.

*...fucking crazy. like there'd be blood. eighteen hours. jesus. i scrubbed it all off and no one sees that my hands shake. i don't see them shake. i feel them shake and every time it's a miracle. every time it goes well i say "thank god," or "thank satan" or...who do i thank when the kid's been shot and he'd just killed the other kid who died in the next room on my table? do i thank anyone for that? why is the sun bright like this? like knives slicing through my irises. like the burning knuckles of god grinding my eyes into my skull. noogies from on high. punishing me. punishing me because i'm weak and my hands shake. oh god why do my hands shake so bad? i've seen blood. i never got sick about the blood. it moved so fast, ricocheting off beverly's scrubs. hemostat slips from my fingers, beverly calls out and her eyes flash side to side to see who noticed her eyes flashing side to side...*

The door to the café opens and the server emerges. Her apron is coffee colored. The logo is script. Her breasts are small and he casts his eyes down as she secures the paper cup with the sleeve in his hand.

3

The sleeve's logo runs into the logo on her apron which runs into her dark eyes, like coffee colored aprons on mornings that are too bright. His eyes move up, just a second of sunlight; a slap, really. They water as he thanks her and her pony tail waves good-bye to him as she pivots around to walk into the cafe.

*...she checked me out, didn't she? probably the scrubs. big-time ER doctor. right, huh? such bullshit. no, no, you don't know that. maybe she saw my fucking hands shake. maybe she wonders why the kid died. maybe he didn't have to because of my shaky hands. maybe she isn't the only one who notices. maybe beverly's eyes flashed side to side because of my shaking hands. no one has to know. no one will ever know. and i can stop taking my medicine just like that and then i'll bleed on a table and beverly'll call out when my blood soaks her face. jesus, what's wrong with me? i need to sleep. that's it. i just need to sleep. and i ordered a double shot of espresso because, genius that i am, i have to be ready. huh. what do you have to be ready for, you asshole? doesn't matter. it's better than not waking up. you don't know though, do you...you always wake up and that kid, he'll never wake up again. doesn't matter. my hands don't shake so bad. right. just...right. gotta sleep now. eighteen hours...too fucking long. too long, too bright. i'll come back here when i've been to bed and see if she remembers me, see if she notices my hands.*

# GodIsNowHere

I usually take my phone or at least a book to the beauty salon. I operate under the sublimely compassionate theory that a twenty-something-year-old working through the dizzying physics string theory that is my hair would not want to converse with me as well. Talk about adding insult to injury.

On the day in question, I left my tome at home, my phone in the car. The magazines they had at the salon had the literal capability of sucking the intelligence out of my head the moment I opened them. I'm fairly certain I'd lost all of my third-grade mathematics education. Ergo, the only practical thing to do was to sit in silence and hope I didn't understand my stylist's under-her-breath cursing at my rag-a-mop hair. She held her tongue; I made a note of it and planned to add $3.50 to her tip. She smiled at me encouragingly as my cowlick defied her time and time again. I added another $5.

Soon, another client pulled into the chair next to mine. She twittered about how she did *not* want her hair, sounding very similar to an unrelenting truck reverse sensor. As she spoke, she looked at me and smiled with an unmistakable dimple deepening the grin; she held my gaze and I knew then and there that I was in for conversation, whether I liked it or not.

Once her ample bottom fully settled in, she smiled even brighter and began regaling the entire room—in a fairly penetrating soprano voice—with tales of the sermon she'd heard the previous Sunday. Her hair stylist patted her shoulder as she spoke, then left for the back room to mix her color. My stylist had my string-theory hair to solve, so her attentions were elsewhere.

I was alone with her.

I decided that although my general maladaptive and misanthropic tendencies had thus far served me well, I would pretend that on some level I was listening to her. I'm a bitch, but I'm not so heartless as to let a good sermon rendition go unnoticed. I smiled and nodded and tried to dissuade my eyes from darting around the room for any sort of reading material into which I could insert my nose. I would have, at that juncture, sacrificed my fourth-grade mathematics. Who needs fractions, anyway?

To my horror, I became cognizant that the woman had asked me a question.

"Excuse me?" I smiled and raised my eyebrows, hoping to entice the illusion that I was hard of hearing. Oh, how I wished I was hard of hearing.

"You aren't, are you?"

"Aren't...?"

"Mormon. Sorry...*LDS*."

"Oh, uh...no, I'm not."

"Good! I didn't want to offend you. I'm Catholic and frankly, I just don't understand Mormons at all."

I open my mouth and speak. Massive, gut-broiling, tear-inciting blunder approaching...

Nnnnnnnnnnnnnnnow.

"Why is that?"

Oh God, I wanted to take it back. Why couldn't I take it back? I vowed that I would stop being an atheist if I could just take it back.

But there *is* no god.

"Ha!" She snorked. (No, "snork" is not a word, and yes, she snorked.) "*Did you know* that they think Our Father actually did *you-know-what* with Our Blessed Virgin?"

Now, important side note: I *was* a Mormon. At one point in my life. Growing up in Utah, one had as much luck avoiding that land mine as becoming a pregnant child-bride in Arkansas. I didn't tell her this

6

info-nugget because a) I didn't want to, and b) I didn't want to. I mean, what could I say? She wasn't far off the mark.

I made my, "Oh, I didn't know you could do that with turnips, how interesting" face, and nodded. I wasn't sure how to discourage her. I didn't want to encourage her. Her stylist had yet, at this moment, to return. Time, it seemed, was not on my side. I zeroed in on my stylist's eyes and pierced her concentration with what I hoped was an impassioned stare, coupled with a mild, pleading expression. The apologetic shrug of her shoulders told me I was on my own.

The woman continued. "I mean, can you imagine? The utter.... perversity of the...and that Our Blessed Mother Mary had other children?"

I open my mouth—again, and speak. Massive, gut-broiling, tear-inciting blunder approaching...

Nnnnnnnnnnnnnnnnnnnnnnnnnnnnnnnnnow.

"Oh, like that movie!" My eyes flew open in terror at my own voice.

(I had, of course projectile-vomited this comment referring to the half-assed movie attempt at depicting the half-assed writing attempt of the book *The Da Vinci Code*.)

I hung my head in utter disgust with myself. My stylist shook her perfectly coiffed noggin as if to say, "You're bringing this allllll on yourself."

I sighed, and like the Jesus of myth and religion, hung my head, awaiting the sentencing for my stupidity. (I mean, who walks around claiming to be a king in old-school Jerusalem? Them's fightin' words, so I'm told.)

The woman had partially turned in her chair, a look of vicious horror on her face. "That man's going to *Hell*, that man who wrote that book."

"Well," I said haltingly, "He won't be lonely, what with all the Mormons down there."

Mostly, I just wanted it to stop. For the life of me, I couldn't figure out how to make that happen. Usually I'm a gold-medalist at shutting a person down, replete with an awkward "hrrumph" and a stammer or three. This day? Nothin'. *This* day, I manage to say anything and

7

everything to goad her on.

"Yes, I know. And I hear they don't even believe in Hell, the Mormons. In *Hell*! Can you believe it?"

I smile, shrug, and blink rapidly. "It's—it's crazy."

Now. My stylist. Bless her heart. She was obviously not pumping on all cylinders that day. That, or she has a death wish. She slapped my shoulder lightly, chucking and said—ALOUD, mind you: "What are you talking about? You're an Atheist!"

Our eyes met, my stylist's and mine, and there was an unspoken... moment. Several moments that spoke an infinity of volumes lapsing across time. I know that in *my* volume, her life ended badly. Horribly, actually, with pain, blood, and several inner-ear punctures. I saw her eyes beg me for mercy. I saw her lips curl and wriggle in un-uttered, yet beseeching appeals for absolution. Clemency. Acquittal. At the very least, the entreaty that I would continue to be her client.

I was not feeling particularly filled with mercy. At all.

Until...

I met the woman's gaze. Her eyes ran the gamut from dull realization to horror to what can only be described as teeny-tiny slits filled with putrid disgust. Her mouth opened and her large, ruby-red-outside-but-pale-pink-on-the-inside-where-she'd-been-smacking-them lips seemed to reach over to me, snuggle up close to my ear, and breathe into it ever-so softly:

"Well, you're going to Hell, *too*."

Like a busy carpenter late for a strip-club peep show, her lips retracted like a measuring tape and her eyes glazed over. Her entire being shifted away from me and my ears were blessed, sanctified, and anointed with the sacred sounds of silence.

Again, my stylist's eyes met mine and she smiled a knowing smile and winked. Her moment of repentance had morphed into an opportunistic reveling in her fortuitous assistance.

I didn't care if she planned it. I didn't even care if she took the ingenious way out to stay in my good graces. I think I might have even teared up a little.

8

My stylist's tip was $50 and she had my hair for life. That, and my unequivocal pledge that I would never, ever be tomeless again.

# Salient

The night was sepia.

Usually nights are not sepia, they're salient, that is to say, the city lights create the blackest black and the colors gleam like emblazoned gems. *Salient distinction.* Nights in the city contrast with the neon glow of life, which stubbornly surges forward despite the darkness. In the country, the glow of stars are only the smallest night lights, glowing amid nothingness, urging half-closed eyelids to sleep.

I'm always on the lookout for sepia nights. My father told me that these nights exist, but are only visible on rare occasions, occasions that have an augur of impending misfortune.

"Forget the ring around the moon nonsense," he'd tell me. "Watch for sepia nights." Only when I was old enough to understand did he tell me why, and even then, I'd never been able to fully apprehend the mixture of horror and wonder that danced in his eyes. How could I? I had never seen war.

Therefore, with the night being sepia, I ought to have been more vigilant as I drove home from the gym.

It had been a long day at work and I was exhausted, but if I don't run at least once a day, I feel off-kilter, out of sorts. I feel like I'm colored in sepia, in a way. Even my face seems to have the somber cast upon it.

Since my father moved in with us a year-and-a-half ago, I've felt like I had four children instead of three. It wasn't that Dad needed that much care or attention. But he was a responsibility; he was someone else waiting for me at home while I was off doing one thing or another.

And he never answered the damn phone, so he'd just sit and worry if I was late. He wasn't a burden—I want to make that clear. He helped me and Richard when we were working late by getting the kids to do their homework. Dad had been a sergeant.

As he aged, Dad lost the ability to ascertain whether a story from his days in Britain during WWII was appropriate for the children. One such story had my daughter up half the night. She was in first grade when he'd told her of how, on September 7th, 1940, the blitz had electrified the sepia night with screams, mayhem, explosions so deafening as to puncture an eardrum. My daughter, Anna, had not been able to sleep because an erupting eardrum sounded positively terrifying to her. Her small hands and arms had to be pried off of her head.

My day had been long and strenuous, but even so, I went for a brief run. The air singed my lungs as I walked from the gym where the safe, pedestrian treadmills mitigated the dangers of a woman running alone in the dark of night.

As I drove home, part of me was already there and my heart warmed before my hands could as I thought of the fire blazing, my father listening to Anna spell out her spelling words. I wondered if Richard had arrived home yet and had started dinner. I almost reached for my phone when something on the highway darted in front of my speeding car. I jerked the car to the left, screaming "Oh God!" as I swerved directly toward a black and white cat. It was mostly black, and I swear I saw its eyes before I struck the hind part of him.

I watched him tumble from the blow of my car, and the urge to cry overtook me as I stared in the rearview mirror, sick with grief. The creature sped away into the bushes off of the road where he'd come from. Amid furtive sobs and shaking limbs, I drove all the way to the next light before whipping my car around and going back.

I walked back and forth along the shoulder, straining my eyes in the dark, honing in on any sound that might be a suffering animal. There was nothing—no sound save the cars whizzing by me in their hurry to arrive at their destinations.

When I walked into the house, Richard saw me first. He raced to me and held me, alarmed, asking me what had happened. My sobs were still fresh, but as the warmth of my house surrounded me and the sound of my children's voices, safe in their rooms trickled out, I felt slightly foolish at what seemed suddenly an overreaction.

"It's nothing. Nothing. Just emotional, that's all."

Richard patted me, all too willing to let that be my answer. My father had walked in and I knew he'd know different. I was just like my mother.

After dinner, as Richard put the children to bed, I cleaned up under Dad's astute gaze.

"Night's sepia." He was sitting at the bar in front of me eating his usual—unsalted sunflower seeds. He'd leave a small pile on the counter, which drove me insane, even though he'd always clean up every last one of the shells when he was done.

I glanced up at him and the tears I had so effectively staunched burned in my eyes again without warning.

"What happened tonight?" he asked. His translucent eyes focused sharply on me and I shook my head, smiling, attempting to make light of it and knowing it wasn't light to me at all.

"Well, Dad, it's crazy. I—I hit a cat with my car. I tried to find it, you know, to... Anyway, it was gone."

Dad chewed his seeds and stared at an unspecified spot on the wall in back of me. Finally he nodded, spitting the seed husks out and dithering them onto the tile with his fingers. Our eyes met and his eyes had that look, that knowing. His eyes held the horror and wonder of so many war stories regaled to me throughout my life. My body broke out into uncomfortable chills. Without warning, his eyes returned to normal, like a faucet had turned off the horror.

"Well," he sniffed, "you drive long enough, bound to kill a cat or two."

I nodded my head with him, even though tears trickled down my face. He continued eating seeds and soon, wordlessly, he slid from the stool and cleaned the seeds from the counter. Wiping his hands on his pants, he shuffled down the hall to his room.

12

I wanted to feel better, but his words did little to assuage the ache within me. Then I recalled his eyes that, only moments ago, had had that salient quality. Like a night with no sepia. Like a night with no bombs erupting, bursting the eardrums of the children in their beds.

# Moment

When the gentleman finished combing the sparse strands of hair across his head, mottled with liver spots and freckles, he put on his hat. He always wore a hat to cover his head, and Alma used to laugh at him when he'd take so much time to comb his hair.

*You're wearing a hat, Gil,* she'd say. He reminded her he was a gentleman and if he were to encounter a lady, he'd be obliged to remove it. Her chuckle had been low and melodic, calibrated like a clock. He would always follow up his jests with a kiss to her hand. Alma had always been a lady, his lady, and the house didn't smell the same now. Before, it had a perfumed smell- a powdery finish, as if the dust particles themselves carried her essence in them. Now it smelled like macaroni that's cooked too long. That, and something sour.

The front living room glowed with diffused light through the sheer drapes that he never opened anymore. He glanced up at the heavier blue curtains, hung like tapestries to guard the window. He wondered how Alma had ever been able to dust atop the mysterious square boxes housing the hooks. The light was not unpleasant, but still too bright, and he knew it would be raw and sharp outside. The day was spring-like so he donned his hat. The walk wasn't far.

He didn't like carrying the plastic shopping bag. It made him feel like a pauper. He didn't like the sound it made against his leg, like rain pelting harshly against glass during a storm, like a storm in the spring when there ought to be sun. Like days when men bury their wives and can't hold the umbrella against the storm any longer. No, he didn't like the spring rains at all. And he didn't like to look like a pauper.

14

The only other bag he had was slightly less dignified. Alma had carried her church music in it. The bag was bright green and had a felt tree on the front with fuzzy pink pom-pom apples. He had teased her about it when she'd made it-she insisted they were blooms. He always called it her *pink apple bag* and her laugh floated through his ears as imaginary rain pelted glass against his leg while he walked down the street to the shoe repair shop.

His shoes were Florsheim's and had smart stitching across the toe and up the sides. The sole was coming apart around the heel. He only wore them to Sunday services, but he'd had them for years. They were timeless. They would always be good shoes for Sundays.

He shuffled along the sidewalk and watched the bicycles whiz by him with mild amusement. Today the bicycles and their riders seemed like they were all in a hurry. When he was a boy, he'd ridden his bike with relish, just to ride.

At the front entrance to the shoe repair shop he paused; the lights were off. He didn't have his watch but couldn't see why they'd be closed so early in the afternoon unless, of course, it was for lunch. He moved closer to the door and placed his hand, dry and soft, against the side of his face to quiet the burgeoning brightness of the afternoon's light.

The thing he noticed first was his heartbeat, how it slowed but seemed to beat with renewed strength. His breath fogged up the glass so he pulled back slightly and waited for his vision to adjust to the darkened alcove. The wall of the shop still had metal hangers jutting from the slats with insoles and Dr. Scholl's orthopedic inserts. The shoeshine kits and polish lay askew on the floor, like a miniature storm had blown through and toppled the bottles upon each other.

He touched the cold brass handle of the door and tugged. It didn't budge. Another bicyclist rode by and he felt the wind on his hand. The boy on the bike said something to him in Spanish, but he didn't understand, so he continued gazing inside the window as if he'd never heard it. The light from the sun hovered brighter now and it streamed into the shop, a diffused light creating dancing dust particles inside the beams. After a moment, he knew: it wasn't lunch time and no one would return.

The grocery bag seemed very heavy in his hand then, and he turned and gazed down the street, squinting, wondering where he could go with his Florsheim shoes. He knew that these days, people just bought new shoes. It's what his son had told him. But he didn't think that was useful or grateful. *You ought to be grateful for good shoes*, he'd told him. His son had sighed and it sounded like he'd patted him on the head over the phone, which made him excuse himself quickly and hang up. Now he peered down the sidewalk and realized he had no idea what lay beyond the next streetlight anymore.

He continued to watch as the sun warmed the back of his neck, and he heard voices in back of him. The voices were female and their conversation moved quickly away from him as they passed by him to stand at the corner and wait for the light.

The light going north was red. He stared ahead, looked back at the abandoned shop, and then down at his grocery bag. Then the light, it changed and turned green and the pedestrians, they began to walk.

# Patch Kit

It's not supposed to sound that way, you see."

The young man looked up with only his eyes as he held the bicycle bell.

Rrrrinngggg!

Rrrrinnggg!

"It sounds like a bicycle bell, Ma'am."

The young man's voice wobbled, as if his certainty was suddenly misplaced. A bigger man, bigger in the sense that he walked with the authority of One Who Knows, approached. The young man's shoulders visibly relaxed, as if a giant bicycle bell had been lifted from them.

"Let me help Mrs. Appleton, Trevor. You help this customer over here." (Louder): "Trouble with the bicycle bell again, Mrs. Appleton?"

By the time Trevor got to me, his face had a flush creeping halfway up. The other half was glasses.

"Hello, can I help you?" He used his middle finger to push his specs up by the bridge. I wanted to warn him about that, but he wasn't my kid.

"Yes, thank you…I need a patch kit."

"Okay, uh, what color?"

"Flesh? Do you have flesh color?"

"'Flesh?'"

"You know, Caucasian."

"We have black and clear and I think white—"

"I'll take pink, even, or peach."

"Uh…"

"Brown?"

The manager had convinced Mrs. Appleton that her bell sounded just as it should, because as she shuffled away, he approached.

"Did you say a patch kit?"

He had the authority. He would understand.

"Yes, flesh colored."

His brows knitted. I became impatient.

"You know, flesh? Caucasian?"

"What do you need to patch?" he asked.

It was at this sublime moment when I realized with a discomforting jolt, that I wasn't in Kansas anymore. Or I was. I was, I definitely was… but where I had been living was nowhere near this town, this bike shop, or the two people staring at me.

*

It started when I married my husband, Steve. To get really technical about it. The long and short of it was that we married, we bred, we succeeded in getting them all out of the house, and then…something happened to me.

I was lying in bed reading, and a sensation that had only tickled me a few times in our marriage came, unbidden, unexpected, and exploded over and through me before I could even utter a sound.

"Jan? What's wrong?" Steve's query came from a mouth full of toothpaste, and the faucet ran a steady stream of ice cold water. I wanted to tell him that was wasteful, like I do every night, but I couldn't catch my breath.

"Jan? You okay?"

Was I okay? The second I squeezed my thighs together I was okay one more time.

"Honey?" I knew he was really concerned because he spit his toothpaste wad out before asking. I finally found my voice.

"I can't believe what just happened! And this book is non-fiction!"

"What?"

My sexual awakening at the age of 48 appeared without warning, and without warning I was not the person Steve had married twenty-seven years ago.

He accused me of trying to kill him on several occasions. A trip to our family doctor, and Steve had an awakening of his own.

The honeymoon was on full-force. I was insatiable. I began buying lingerie to greet him in when he got home from work. I discovered Internet Porn. I became a statistic.

One day at lunch, I confessed my newfound obsession to my girlfriend Beth.

"And I want more. I even bought a vibrator."

Beth, who had long-since discovered her own bodily needs—although not nearly as voraciously as I, revealed something to me—a fact she had hidden from me successfully for five out of the fifteen years of our friendship. I was pretty sure a bird could have nested in my mouth in the time it took me to close it.

"Swingers?"

"We've been doing it for five years. It's ramped up our sex life twenty-fold."

Twenty-fold.

That duet of words echoed inside my entire being, like a mystical calling to a Hobbit.

She invited us to a party the following Saturday evening.

"You can just watch. You don't have to do anything," she assured me with outstretched palms.

I politely declined and had an orgasm on the way home following a semi-intentional swerve onto the highway rumble strips.

My heart was beating under my ribs—a racket, a reminder of every word Beth had uttered to me. Well, two words. And a hyphen. Twenty-fold.

I could barely look Steve in the face when he got home. I felt I was keeping something precious from him, something he ought to know, now that I was privy to it.

I had to pace myself with him. Over the past three months, Steve had been thrilled with my newfound—oh, let's face it, first-time obsession with All Things Sexual. Before, sex had been snuck up on me, like a wrinkle you don't notice until you're in a public restroom. Steve could catch me off-guard if I was extra sleepy, or in some cases, sick and on cold medicine. It's not that I was frigid. I just had better things to do, like sleep and eat and take care of four children. I knew Steve had needs. Hell, we all have needs. But his needs seemed to coincide with my utterly different needs more often than not; that, or I was monumentally blind.

That night, I saw him pop a blue pill and I instinctively squeezed my thighs together. This is what I had done for twenty-seven years. The result was not what it used to be. I panted on the bed and Steve poked his head out to look at me.

"Wow! Already starting without me?" He walked into the bedroom, face beaming, pleased as punch.

"I didn't mean to. And anyway, I have to talk to you."

He peeled off his robe revealing his tall frame, once athletic and sinewy, now a little less formed, a little more uniform. Where shoulders had tapered into a small waist, the effect was more like a fleshy rectangle, a block of ice with brown arms, tanned from the golf course and lawn mowing. He began to move his hips sensually and instead of responding with my usual aerial leg-V, I suppressed a giggle. He put his hands on his hips.

"You said you liked that—"

"No, no, no, that's not it. I had lunch with Beth today."

"Oh yeah?"

"I—we…were invited to a party Saturday night."

"Oh yeah? A barbeque?"

"No."

I didn't want to screw it up. Part of me was ready to let him decide. If I left it up to him, he'd do the right thing, whatever that was. I knew which way I leaned. Twenty-fold degrees to the left.

"Well what then?"

"An adult party. Like with swingers. Like on the movies we watch." I whispered the last portion because we still hadn't openly discussed my porn proclivity.

I scoured his face for an expression I could decipher, but it was void of everything familiar to me. After twenty-seven years, that worried me a little. Finally:

"You…you want to do…that?"

Was that a twinge of hurt in his left eye? Did the corner of his mouth tremble slightly? Did I see a nostril redden?

"Well only if you do—" but my body betrayed me and I climaxed with crossed eyes and one leg spazzing uncontrollably in the air. "S-s-sorry…"

"Oh, wow. I mean…I hadn't ever thought about it really."

I folded my arms over my newly-flushed chest. "You're telling me you have never, ever entertained the idea of having sex with someone besides me."

"Well…yeah, I mean, no, not like that…"

But his body betrayed him, too.

"Ah-HA!" I pointed, and he covered himself like a virginal nymph.

"It's the pill!" he said, sweat gracing his upper lip.

"Liar. It doesn't bother me, Steve."

"It doesn't?"

"No. No it doesn't…"

But suddenly, it did. My mind had only skated over the surface of all of the implications. Mostly it had skated over what I would be doing. Or who I'd be doing. The implications of what swapping partners would entail for both of us washed over me, and it was in fleshy, living color underneath my husband's meaty palms.

"Because I know it wouldn't bother me—you with someone else, I mean." He said this quickly, as if to reassure me. His eyes were a tad wide and suddenly his palms weren't large enough.

"No?" I asked.

"No! I mean, you love me, right?"

"Of course I do."

"So it would just be like when you use your vibrator-thingy."

"My 'vibrator thingy' is blue with bubble-gum beads and a bunny. Hardly realistic."

"It's phallic."

"Not as phallic as a phallus, Steve!"

"Why are you upset with me? I thought—"

"Oh, it's not you…it's me. I don't know what I was thinking! I don't know if I could."

He smiled and moved toward me. "You know you're all I've ever needed. I'm content with that."

It was a sweet sentiment.

Content.

Twenty-fold.

Those three words (and the hyphen) danced in and out of me for a good fifteen minutes before we both fell into an exhausted but restless sleep.

*

Three shipping nights later, Steve did not come home to me in a baby doll and high heels. He came home to Rita.

"What do you think?" I stood in our bedroom, admiring my work.

"You-what-you-what-"

"I embellished. She didn't come with hair originally."

I held the blow-up doll under her arms in front of me, as if I showed him my new craft project.

"See, I added the blond wig—" (I'm a red-head) "-and the nipples-" (she originally didn't have any),"-and I even glued some pubic hair here—"

"Jan! Are you crazy? She's plastic! I mean, what in the world am I supposed to do with her?"

"I call her Rita. I think that's a sexy name, Rita. Don't you? Anyway, her mouth is an opening—"

"Jan—"

"—and there are two more down here—"

22

"Jan! Are you listening to me! Are you listening to yourself?"

"What?"

"What am I supposed to do with it?"

"Her."

"Her, it, whatever! I can't possibly. I mean…it's a pathetic…it's…"

"Oh, so my vibrator makes me pathetic?"

"I didn't say that. I like you…with that."

"Well I like you with Rita."

His shoulders sagged. His moments of defeat came so much quicker than they had ten years ago. He placed his hand on top of his head and for the first time, he really looked at her.

"Hair's nice."

"You like it? I got it at Kauffman's Wigs. It cost more than the doll!"

"Oh, Jesus, how much—"

"Don't talk about her like we bought her! She's no whore."

"Jan…"

"Take a pill, please? If I see you with her and I'm okay, I can see you with a real person and I'll be okay. Okay? Please?"

"You have to help me, because she won't, uh, do it for me alone."

"Oh, I plan on being here the whole time." I put on my sexiest face and he smiled. He still didn't seem to want to make eye contact with Rita, which I thought was a little rude.

He came out of the bathroom and I had Rita all ready for him. I was actually getting into quite a lather thinking about it, which was encouraging.

"Could you turn her over?"

"It's because I don't like anal, isn't it? You want to try anal. Rita will do anal."

"No! I just…the face is a little disconcerting."

I looked at her pretty, blue, screen-printed eyes and detected a small trace of sadness.

I picked her up and placed her face down. "Happy now?"

Steve shot me a look.

After configuring some good Internet porn on the laptop, which

23

entailed placing Rita across the bed rather than vertically on it, we were on our way. Steve focused on the laptop screen as the bed bounced away, and I focused on her hair, her head bobbing incessantly up and down as if she were eternally trying to flip her hair to give it body.

The sensations and emotions were undeniable. I had an inkling, a small taste of twenty-fold as I watched with wide eyes and furious curiosity.

But I was not the only curious one in the room.

Unknown to Steve and me, we had a Watcher, and we hadn't anticipated the reaction all of the commotion would cause.

With an unholy screech, our part-cat, part-evil garden gnome leapt from under the bed and gripped Rita's hair with ferocity.

"Stinker! No! Bad kitty!" I gasped.

Steve hated being nude in front of the cat. He said he felt vulnerable with all of the claws. I think it's because the cat's a boy.

Steve immediately got in defensive pose, meaning he jumped off of Rita and collided with the wall. Before I could grab Stinker, he climbed up her head and ran, claws in full-grip mode, down the length of her body. The bursting noises were stomach-churning.

Stinky ran from the room and I watched in horror as Rita aged rapidly before my eyes, sinking into the bed as if she were a witch doused in water.

"Oh no!" I cried.

"Is he gone?" The wall muffled Steve's voice. I turned angrily toward him.

"Some protector you are! What if it had been me?"

He glanced back at me. "Have you ever seen those claws?"

"Oh Rita…" I turned her over, but only the top part of her form twisted. She was all but deflated, a non-living, non-breathing Dorian Gray version of her former self.

"Well, I guess that's that." Steve shrugged, still facing the wall.

"No, it most certainly isn't. I spent all afternoon making her pretty, and I paid good money for her. I'm going to fix her."

"Can we fix me first?" Steve turned around. I squeezed my thighs together. Rita rested comfortably on the floor that night.

\*

"What am I patching?" I repeated the manager's question again.

"Yes, Ma'am. What are you patching?"

I was so tempted. Why should I be the only one with an awakening? Why should I be so selfish? Who knows what might turn this poor man's life around? Perhaps he even has a Rita of his own.

"A chair. A child's pink blow-up chair."

"I see. I can only offer clear patches. They will be a bit shiny, but they'll do the trick."

"Say, do you have any patches that look like tattoos?"

I realized right then that I would never be in Kansas, not ever, ever again.

# Pole

*lick, click, click, click.*

    She hears footsteps on the pale wood floor, but she doesn't look up. She thought everyone had left the studio—in fact, she is sure of it. Maybe Melody hadn't locked the front door. Without looking up, she calls out.

We're *closed.*"

The footfalls stop. She stuffs a towel into her gym bag, white chalk handprints ghostly on the black canvas.

*Click, click, click.*

She reaches in her bag for her pepper spray and lifts her chin, her eyes leading the way. At first the figure before her doesn't make sense. She glances around and then down at the sensible shoes with stable square heels.

"Yes, I see you're closed. But I had a question about taking classes."

Still squatting, Robin blinks twice before answering. "Classes?"

"Yes, you teach the pole dancing classes here?"

"Yeah?"

The woman's face breaks into a smile. "I would like to learn."Robin's legs cramp, with sharp pains shooting up her left knee. Jeez, she didn't need this tonight. She winces and stands up, still wearing her clear, plastic, platform stripper heels. She towers over the tiny woman by a foot. Her hand automatically moves to her hip and she bends a knee.

"Are you kidding me?"

"I most certainly am not."

Robin recognizes the stony look of a school teacher from the woman's face. She involuntarily looks at the woman's arms. Loose skin hangs around her frail upper arms; age spots cover her hands. She couldn't be younger than seventy. Ruth's face hardens determinedly and she "*ehems*."

"Well...okay, sure. Class schedules are on the wall over by the desk."

The woman blinks her eyes quickly. "I can't take a class with a bunch of young girls, obviously."

Robin lifts her leg and crosses it over her thigh to pull her shoe off. Weary from the night of teaching, she clears her throat, determined to nip this old bloom in the bud.

"I don't do privates."

"If I pay you, would you consider it?"

"Everyone pays—"

"I'll pay more."

Their eyes meet. Suddenly a yawn overtakes her and she covers her mouth with the back of her hand. When she dances on weekends, her night would have only just begun in the dim-lit, bass-infused club. Irked at the old woman's determination, she huffs out a breath.

"My only nights off are Wednesdays."

"That'll be fine."

"N—you—I mean, it's my night *off.* And the studio closes at *nine.*"

The woman smiles and lines, like ancient striated stone, deepen and crisscross at her forehead and cheeks. "Nine p.m. would work perfectly. You do own this studio, do you not?"

"Yeah, but—"

"So I can meet you here at nine tomorrow night."

Robin's mouth hangs open slightly.

"Careful, you'll get a fish hook caught in that. What's your name, please?"

"Robin. Robin Morris."

"Ruth Patterson." Ruth says this with a curt nod. She glances around, eyes glassy and translucent. Her scalp shows through her sparse, steel gray hair.

Robin glances down at her keys, poised on the floor, ready to take her home to the empty house. Blue eyes stare at her from her key chain. Her son might still be up and she could call him. *If* his father and step-bitch let him talk. *If* this old bag hadn't kept her too long.

Ruth stoically stands in front of her, and Robin sniffs.

"So, can I ask how old you are?"

Ruth's eyebrows rise slightly. "I don't know. Can you?"

*Definitely a school teacher.*

"What I *mean* is, pole training isn't for everyone, Ruth."

"Mrs. Patterson. And I'm sure it's not."

"The classes get full...of young girls."

"Hence the private instruction."

Robin exhales impatiently. Ruth pivots on her heel to leave.

"Hey, can I—*may* I ask you something, Mrs. Patterson?"

The old woman's mouth almost twitches into a half-smile. "You may."

"Are you doing this to work out?"

"Heavens, no." Her clear gray eyes pierce the distance between them and without another word, Ruth shuffles to the door.

*One spin on the pole, the old hag'll give up.* Robin follows behind the woman and watches her as she steps to her car.

*

It had been four weeks, and tonight is her fifth class. Ruth is late. Robin stands by the front door and peers up and down the street, breath fogging up the glass. Soon she sees Ruth's old Plymouth pull up to the curb.

"I apologize for being tardy."

"It's alright." Robin holds the door open for the old woman, who shrugs off her coat. They walk into the studio, where Ruth kicks off her slip-on shoes.

The music echoes off of the walls, but soft, as Ruth doesn't like it to "blow out her ear drums." Robin does a full spin on the pole and spins all the way to the ground. She rests her head on the icy metal. Ruth's voice punctuates the music.

"That boy on the key chain yours?"

Robin's gut tightens and she pulls herself closer to the pole, as if it will protect her insides. "Yes."

"Does your husband stay with him while you're here?" Ruth's eyebrows, darkened in with pencil, rise expectantly.

"He—he lives with his dad, who's married now. We—we weren't..."

"I see. I pried and I shouldn't have." Ruth's mouth moves to a straight line and almost turns down at the corners. Her eyes blink rapidly and Robin releases her death-grip on the pole.

"You didn't pry. It's okay. I was into some bad things when he was little. I made a lot of mistakes."

"We all make those."

"Well mine made me lose my son."

Ruth watches silently as Robin's face mirrors events that have long since passed, events that flash across and through her eyes like spikes.

"Well, Robin, I believe I'm ready to do that spin." Glad for the reprieve, Robin stands and sweeps her hand to the pole.

"Be my guest."

Ruth steps close to the pole and clenches her eyes tight. Both hands grip, knuckles white on the metal, and she hugs it almost to her cheek. She wraps one leg around and slides down, barely turning around it once. When her eyes open, she's on the floor. Her face breaks into a grin. "That...was spectacular!"

Her hand reaches up for Robin's and Robin helps her stand. Robin tries to hold back a smile, but it breaks through.

"You did really good."

"'Really *well*.'"

"Right. *Well*."

"You're a fine teacher."

"Oh...thanks."

"And I appreciate your indulgence."

Robin's smile fades. "You're coming back, right?"

"I did what I came here to do, I suppose. It's not every day a seventy-four-year-old dances on a pole."

29

"But—but you have a lot more you can learn, Mrs. Patt—"

"*Ruth*. And let's face it, Robin. We can only stay away from our empty houses for so long."

Robin peers into Ruth's eyes and sees the nights, long and dark, staring at a ceiling with no shadows. Quiet houses, like deathly still echo chambers, which await each turn of the dead bolt from within. The final turn and click reverberate throughout the house, the night, and well into morning.

Robin blinks fast and a wan smile appears. "Maybe tonight we'll sleep."

Ruth's smile is wry. "Perhaps."

"So...see you next week?"

Ruth nods her head once. She turns on the pale wood floor and walks across it into the dark.

# The Spring War

This story is really a Christmas story, or perhaps it's a family story. It could even be a story of the ages, a story of boy meets girl, boy marries girl, they go on to have four children and...an all-out war every spring. Or maybe it's my story, the story of the second youngest daughter and the day she earned her rightful place in her ubiquitous family from Utah.

As the middle child I was always in "the know." That is to say, I was a fly on the wall rather than a fly in the ointment. I was neither adorably special like the twins, nor the oldest and a high school football *wunderkind* like my older brother. Being eight years younger than him—and a girl, made for some very beige days. The year was 1977 and Gary was the quarterback for Ogden High School's football team—even though he wouldn't be a senior until the next year. They were heading for a great season come fall, and the training started as soon as the ground thawed.

The twins were born when I was six, leaving me to be the perennial babysitter and general do-everythinger, mostly because despite what our church leaders said, my mother worked "outside of the home."

The debate over whether she should go to work was an emotional, sordid affair, with my mother in tears half of the time while my father smashed his fist *just so* into his meaty palm. Other times, my mother pointed her index finger straight up as my father shook his head in resolute stoicism. But one night, on a Monday Family Home Evening, after "hours of thoughtful fasting and prayer," Mother and Dad came to the conclusion that because of the damn Democrats, Mother had to

31

take a job at my elementary school as the school nurse. My first thought had been no more faking sick for me. My second thought was actually handed to me, compliments of Gary.

"That means Mutt will have to get busy and do her share around here."

"Mutt" was the moniker bestowed upon me by Gary and indulged by my mother solely because my father felt Gary was "all boy", and calling me a derogatory name proved it. That, my buck teeth, and glasses the size of Coke bottle bottoms all seemed to prove him right. Mother tied my braids back into a tight line so that my nose seemed to be as wide as it was long. With the all-too-early pre-pubescent pimples poking their white heads up on my nose, I accepted the nickname with only a token objection.

It was during that spring of 1977 when things took an awkward turn in the Hansen Household. Mother had purchased a Crock-Pot, the "cooks all day while the cook's away" gadget, with an orange stoneware crock inside and a mottled beige outer husk that heated it slowly at a low wattage. During this particular energy crisis, we were told by my father to "turn off the lights" as he literally slept in his armchair reading the *Deseret News*. He also told us to wash the cat—but we didn't own a cat. One night my mother was in the kitchen dishing up a slow-cooked concoction with a strange twinkle in her eye. See, there was an unspoken resentment brewing that year because "it" was still on the lawn.

The "it" to which I refer is actually more of a "they." As in a group. Every Christmas, my mother lovingly placed the Nativity scene complete with glowing plastic baby Jesus on our front lawn. My father bragged that he'd built the "stable" himself; the stable consisted of pieces of particle board, "two-buh-fours" holding it up, and straw adhered to it by nail gun and rubber cement. The lumber still had *Burton's Lumber* stamped on it, but Dad said the snow would wash it away. I wonder to this day if it ever did, or if that ink ran as deep as the fissure growing in our happy home.

Every year my parents argued about who would put away the Nativity scene. Every year it sat on our lawn until the sweet buds of spring nosed their way out of winter oblivion. Every year, at the end of an acrimonious argument upstairs, one of them would come downstairs and slam the front door on their way out. The Nativity scene was usually conspicuously gone the next day as we pulled out of the garage to go to school. We all had unspoken knowledge, almost a primordial instinct, if you will, to never speak of it. Thanks to the new working arrangement, both my parents' heads were as bull as bull can be.

That year, in the year of our Lord 1977 A.D., March 1st had come and gone and March 7th was nigh.

My mother had not only been hired on as school nurse, but she'd also taken on the added responsibility of helping my teacher and the other third-and fourth-grade teachers grade papers. The twins were at Sister Finlayson's house, and I was home with my brother, Gary. He had brought home two of his teammates and I stayed hidden, mortified that he'd use my nickname in front of them. I learned early on that invisibility had its perks. "It" still rested on the lawn, and as I crouched behind the sofa in our front living room, I heard my brother and his two friends carousing up from the rec room after inhaling all of the Clover Club potato chips we had in the pantry.

I prayed for continued invisibility, and my prayer was answered as hushed tones and loud guffawing emerged into the room. The front door slammed behind Gary and I sniffed the air for possible threats. I could hear their muffled shouts from outside in the front yard and I slowly peered over the window sill. My eyes grew into saucers of horror.

Gary had plucked the small, plastic baby Jeebus—the name the twins called Him, *off* of the lawn and was hurling *Him*, through the air á la football style, to his friends. My mouth hung open so the window fogged in front of me and I could smell the Freedent gum which had, by then, dropped onto the carpet in my astonishment.

Now, back then, Polaroid cameras were still the rage, and ours was my father's pride and ecstatic joy. In my youth, I had yet to ever hold it. My mother had attempted its use at a church dinner. The result was a photo of half of her eye and a nostril, and a mocking reprimand from my father—I believe the word he employed was "ding-bat." Ergo, my mother didn't bother with the camera again. My father was the only person in the household allowed to wield the Polaroid, and although my early demise should have been foremost on my mind, what was really on my mind was revenge.

I tip-toed up to my parents' room, not knowing the time or how soon before my mother or father would return. My scalp shrank over my skull as my ears honed in on any out-of-the-ordinary sound that might trigger an abortive maneuver. But the coast was clear and I pressed on.

I knew from casual glances and mostly from hanging onto my mother when she ironed, that the camera was in my father's desk in the big drawer.

I opened the drawer and there it sat, in its rigid cardboard box, pristine and ready. I lifted the box, my hands shaking, and I wasn't sure if I imagined a small trickle going down my leg or not. The camera was heavier than it looked. There were 20 pictures left. My father counted. I had to be absolutely sure.

My hands were clammy with perspiration and I knew—*knew* Gary would catch me with the camera heading down the stairs. But as I reached the top of the steps, I could hear them hooting and hollering out in front. They were oblivious. I could only capture snippets of their taunts to each other, but one thing was clear—they had *renamed* Baby Jeebus. They called him BJ.

"Hey Gary, why don't you give Kirk a BJ?"

"Hey Kevin, I heard you give great BJs."

I didn't understand the special significance of this new moniker for Baby Jeebus, but their salacious laughter told me it was something to file in my fly-on-the-wall files.

I walked to the window, pointed, and clicked.

The camera spat out my prize and I waved it like my father did, measured and precise. Like a ghostly apparition, the images appeared. The picture was perfect. Had it not been Baby Jeebus, my father would have been so proud of Gary's form.

The photo paper was still wet, but I ran upstairs, almost dropping

34

the camera twice as my breath huffed out of me. I replaced the camera, knowing my sweaty fingerprints would be smelled a mile away on its black-and-white plastic surface.

Then, I prayed.

*

That night at dinner, the air was heavier than normal. I didn't care. The lightness in my spirit made up for it—all of it. My mother mumbled under her breath as she cleared the table and my father's head snapped toward her.

"What was that?"

Her tone was even, but her eyes blazed. "I *said* Madge commented on our lawn today at PTA.»

Our lawn, of course, meant "it." Madge, of course, meant the neighborhood and church gossip. The women of the Weber South 12th ward congregation lived in perpetual fear of being the target of her tongue.

"Well, that's too bad. Maybe it should get picked up." My father's cool veneer belied his reddening ears and neck. Madge's husband, Bill, was also my father's supervisor at the accounting firm. My father was playing a dangerous game. We all held our collective breath. Well, Gary and I did. The twins wiped cream of chicken soup heavy with onion flakes in each other's hair.

"Yes, maybe it should. Bill's seen it." My mom did it. She dropped the gauntlet and she dropped it casually. She was almost breezy.

Gary and I glanced at each other and down at our plates. The acrimony would begin tonight.

Without warning, my father parried and dodged.

"Doubt it. He's gone on business."

Mom was ready; she parlayed and went in for the kill. "Saw him this morning. He told me he'd help me take it down." I had been with my mother that morning. No such conversation occurred. Her eyes shot at me to be still, and I was.

My father's entire face took on a purple hue. He was to be the pariah.

35

Another woman's husband offered what my father wouldn't—or couldn't. The ward gossips were having a field day at his expense. He wore his shame like a giant red BJ. He stormed from the room, but his presence lingered there like the Ghost of Christmas Past.

The icy air was only slightly punctuated by the twins' *ABC* song, as Mother hurriedly wiped chicken soup off of their heads with a kitchen towel. She continually glanced my way, furtively, begging my forgiveness with her eyes.

But upstairs, a pot was boiling over.

"*Nineteen!*"

I froze in my spot. My father's voice bellowed from the hallway.

"Who took the Polaroid? I'm missing a picture*! Ninteeeeen*!"

Gary's eyes met mine and his face broke into a cruel grin. He would blame me and it would be believed, mostly because it was true. All of the rancor and ire of the evening would flow onto me, and it would flow like milk and honey. When my face didn't convey abject terror, Gary's smile lost some of its evil.

I had something that only Gary could decipher on my plate.

My green beans clearly and plainly spelled, when turned to face my brother, "B-J." Gary's face fell like a doomed water balloon. His expression dissolved into panic. He shook his head *no* even as my father hollered "Nineteen!" from mid-stair.

Gary continued to shake his head no.

I, in my desperate bravado, nodded *yes*.

Lips firmly pressed tight, my eyes told the whole story and Gary had only one way out. Gary had to create the ultimate diversion—and the ultimate win-win. I've got to give him credit, even today, for the slippery brilliance with which his mind maneuvered that evening.

"I'll do it."

My father stepped into the kitchen and my mother's gaze landed squarely on Gary.

Gary's voice shook slightly. "I'll clean the lawn up. It can be my new job."

My mother had tears of pride in her eyes as my father slapped his

36

oldest son on the back. "Good man, yes, you're a good man, son." Polaroid photo: forgotten. It didn't matter now.

The tension dissipated like a melting fudgsicle and my parents both had a semblance of normal color return to their faces.

They exhaled and shared a private glance of what can only be described by a nine year old as *yuck*, and Gary went to the front yard, without another word. He didn't bother with a parka.

So, I guess I can honestly say that I was saved by Baby Jeebus. If it weren't for his glowing, plastic presence, I would have never shirked the moniker of *Mutt*. And I would have never become one of the most feared persons in the Hansen household. Well, thanks to Jeebus, Polaroid, and Sony.

My brother and parents never did acquire that photo. I was good to my unspoken word. And my mother never found the missing Nativity scene four years later, when it mysteriously disappeared one snowy March evening well after Gary left on his mission.

I caught that one on the new Sony Betacam.

# Yearning

A mildly irritating phenomenon exists in these grocery stores, just as it exists in the quaint little markets around the world: once you begin shopping, there is always a sort of *procession*. The person ahead of you always seems to *be* ahead of you, and no matter how many aisles you skip or which way you choose to point your cart, there they are, drinking in the sight of seventy flavors of jams, jellies, and preserves.

This was so just the other day, when I needed only a small number of items, things to get us through until the next large haul. The day was the first real day of spring, the kind that started with a refreshing chill and the scent of virgin blooms wafting through the air. As the day wore on, the sweaters came off, the windows went down, and the sun shone in a brilliant spotlight over naked shoulders and glistening foreheads.

As I entered the store, the man ahead of me didn't glance my way as he moved toward the produce section. I reasoned my trip would be brief; surely he didn't need produce and items on aisles 3,7,8,14,16, and 23. Yet as I chose grapes, he chose melon. While I selected my lettuce, he fondled and sniffed tomatoes. To my misanthropic dismay, he continued ahead of me as we both wandered toward aisle three.

As I entered the aisle of canned goods, he had stopped, as many are wont to do, right in the center of the aisle. His bald head reflected the great neon lighting of the store. I wondered why he didn't shave his head completely. He was only in his mid- to late thirties and the ring of brown hair reminiscent of a 13th-century monk along with his plaid, short-sleeved button-up shirt aged him. His long, tall frame rendered him as a man who had not excelled in any brute-force sports, but who would perhaps play tennis or golf. Lanky, awkward, someone I would have targeted in high school.

He was not staring at food choices, however. Directly in front of him, two college girls price-checked canned peaches, calculators in-hand for the task.

I grabbed my cans of pineapple and watched as he glanced away from them and then back again, shuffling in an agonizingly slow cadence. The girls had donned their summer clothes-flimsy spaghetti-stringed tanks, bra-straps mismatched and prominent. One had cut-off shorts, revealing smooth, supple skin. The other, a flowing skirt, legs almost visible through the fabric. I caught my shopping partner's profile: beakish nose, deep-set eyes, not unattractive, and not outstanding. The girls were oblivious to anyone else around them as their lilting voices rose up and down like a lover's breath. As I passed them, I noticed the scent of honeysuckle, imagined or not, hovering about. As if the man could feel my presence propelling him forward, he picked up his pace and moved out of the aisle.

I found him again on aisle eight. A young woman with a blonde ponytail squatted on her haunches to choose a baking mix. Her back was exposed, and tendrils of moist hair kissed the back of her bare neck. He chanced to stand near her, placing large hands over small sacks of sugar as if to measure their width with his finger span. The girl, absorbed in her task, didn't glance up. A light sheen of perspiration gleamed on his head and when the blonde moved away with her selection, he patted his crown and watched her with innocuous eyes.

Indeed, the store was a plethora of flowering youth, as if the thawing ground had split open to release Persephone and her maids from the Underworld. Each aisle brimmed with velvety shoulders, fabrics swelling with enticing mounds of creamy flesh, rounded arms and sun-kissed cheeks. A garden of fresh-plucked flowers collected and displayed in a vase of the sparkling, sanitary neon of the store.

For our staggered and uneven partnership, we managed to be in the same checkout queue, flanked by more co-eds, unconscious of the

39

intoxicating attar about them.

I glanced at his wedding ring and the cans of formula on the moving belt as he emptied the scant items from his cart. Nothing in his scrutiny of the girls would have garnered opprobria from anyone. Absent was the lasciviousness of the typical male gaze as he seemed of two minds-watching himself as closely as he watched them.

Even as I followed him toward the exit and his eyes followed one last buttery young woman as she weighed apples in self-checkout, his manner remained reticent and modest.

His car was closer than mine, and I glanced over as he tossed his cache in the rear of his sensible white mid-sized sedan. When he got in the driver's seat he didn't busy himself with his keys, nor did he start his engine. He reached up and tilted the rear-view mirror. I craned my neck, thinking he'd seen another blossoming vision walking toward the store. No one moved behind him and I realized then, he was only gazing at himself.

# Peter Pan for Girls

T he familiarity between the other poets in the room left her devoid of the sense of comity she'd been anticipating. It had been years and she was out of the loop.

She'd written all of her best stuff on napkins in smoky coffee houses, back in the days when smoky coffee houses served coffee black, and only when an amateur arrived did the cream and sugar come out. But that was before, before. Before her life had become a white-bread turkey sandwich. With cheese. She needed some napkins. Or smoke. Or smoke and mirrors. Ah, but she'd had plenty of that.

The last time she went to a coffeehouse to write poetry, she'd brought her pretty bound notebook with a picture of a tree on it. She wondered if that was her problem. Her well-meaning husband got it for her for Mother's Day. It was hard to write *fuck* in a pretty bound notebook. She had ordered a coffee, black, and the barista's forehead had crinkled and she'd shaken her head.

"You want…an Americano?"

*No*, she said, *just coffee*. She realized then that nothing was "just coffee" anymore.

As other poets filed into the small room, a man-boy sat next to her. He wore a top hat, a woman's scarf, and had a pocket watch that he pulled out every 32 seconds until he was sure she saw it. She didn't know if it was an antique or just made to look that way, like so many things. Old is new, young is new, being 40 is being 40.

Then she saw *her*. It had been fifteen years and the woman who breezed into the room looked just the same. How could she look just the same? *Because she hadn't popped out three kids, that's how she looked the same.* She didn't know why her ever-patient husband's voice suddenly taunted her mind.

If Jade was here, if Jade was reading, it wasn't *Open Mic Poetry Nite*, it was *Jade Keller Poetry Nite*. She saw a fingerless glove appear in front of her.

"I'm Logan."

"Oh, hi. Holly." The pocket-watch sat on his lap and she shook his hand, the leather of the glove disturbingly hard and rough.

"I didn't know Jade Keller would be here. She's tight."

Holly wasn't sure if she could agree with Logan on that. She had no idea if Jade was "tight."

She hoped Jade wouldn't see her in the small pond of faces, and she didn't. Holly and Jade had taught poetry workshops together in their twenties, when they were both single, when they both wore silky, diaphanous, tribal print gauzy tops and funky hats. Jade opted for patchouli and hairy armpits, but Holly, selling out to Western ideals, shaved and wore deodorant. She always knew it was just a game. Yet the rules had changed on her while Jade held to the old ways. Her knee-length skirt, funky boots, and mismatched gossamer top, along with her small-brimmed violet velvet hat, sent that message loud and clear, and Holly at once felt strangely garish in her neutrals.

Her little tree notebook sat like a demure child on her lap. She'd planned on reading her poem "Peter Pan for Girls" tonight. Now that Jade was here, her hand weighed heavy and clammy on her book.

In walked an older gentleman, well-known in the poetry community for his performance pieces that often employed onomatopoeias and nonsensical mutterings with hidrotic theatrics. In his late 50s now, he entered the fuggy room holding his well-worn, ancient-looking (on purpose?) leather-bound notebook. His name was Hector. He and Jade had collaborated on a poetry chapbook around the time Holly was planning her all-but-ironic white wedding.

Just as Holly was contemplating the bathing rituals of Allen Ginsberg,

Hector stood without introduction. Everyone clapped, dispersing the body odor and Nag Champa molecules around the room so that she could barely breathe.

As Hector began to sputter and make a low '*ong*' sound in his throat, Holly began small talk in her crowded head.

*How are you?*

*Oh, fine, fine, you?*

*I'm great, yeah…still married?*

*Yeah, three kids now.*

*Oustanding. Yeah, that's great. Good to see you…*

*Yeah, you too. Take care…*

Irked at the racket Hector was sputtering, she opened her book and read through "Peter Pan for Girls" again. She wondered why she couldn't be happy without the shadow of these silver-bangled-gauged-pierced-nomad-patchouli-wearing wanna-be beatniks all lined up the rows (stinking), and wearing each other's clothes that they bought at the local used and vintage shop.

"Fucking *tight*," Logan muttered under his breath.

While the poets in the room were busy getting 'tight' all of these years, Holly was at soccer practice. Holly opened her book and read.

*… when had heroism come in a wooden box,*

*in five-thousand flavors of red, white, and blue?*

*and when did peter pan become a boy?*

*when it was a girl who flew?*

*why isn't there a peter pan for girls?*

*we'll call her Polly Pan…*

Holly clapped on automatic with the rest of the sycophants and watched as Hector handed out tissues to the front row to wipe off their faces. Holly was glad she'd sat three rows back. She wasn't ready for them to call her name. She couldn't swallow.

Jade stood and glided to the podium. She smiled, broad and confident, and began in a southern accent. She wasn't from the south, but her poetry often tussled with the stereotypical Southern Gothic elements that left the listener unsettled and trapped.

As the melodic tempo of Jade's poetry arrested the crowd, Holly found herself restless. Her ass cheeks danced in her chair like her five-year-old's danced at church services. The one thing her husband, Kirk, insisted on—weekly church. Holly agreed because her husband lived with her, a labile, emotional artist who realized that writing poetry was as useful and profitable as the napkins they were written on. Kirk was *practical*. He was a *grown up*, said her mother. Kirk was an engineer. And every poem she read to him, he would smile in that accepting way and say, "I liked it. Very nice." He mustered the same enthusiasm for her cassoulet on their anniversary. But how could he have known she'd worked all day? How could he know of the scarcity of goose at their local butcher's shop?

And he was home with the three children so that she could be here and pretend to be something she wasn't.

*That's fucked up.*

Holly's fingers dance on the tree covering her notebook. Why didn't she have a leather-bound job? A *Moleskine*, for God's sake?

*Yeah, 'cause that makes you legit.*

Holly's breathing nearly doubled back on itself as Jade finished her poem and they announced the next name. The name was not hers and she exhaled and stood, just as Logan told her the next reader was tight.

She hurried out of the room and noticed that the stairs leading her to the next level were fully visible through the all-glass wall behind the podium. On display, running away (to her dismay). Her hand gripped the railing on the stairs in a death-grip, like a blanket in a child's fist. Her legs shook like angry trees, certain she would lose her bearings and tumble down, poetry in motion. Something for the audience to write about as a metaphor for being a chicken shit. Because that's what she was: a chicken shit. She ran away from poetry, ran away from grad school, ran away from a dream because dreams can't pay car payments and aspirations only get in the way of laundry.

*…Polly Pan never grows up, never cuts her hair,*
*she revels in the scent of homemade food her mother makes*
*and she never wonders about those blood covered army boots*

*hiding in the basement under the stairs—*
*boots mother just can't throw away...*

The stairs were never-ending, like a ticker-tape, sprouting steps as she took each one. Fifteen years ago she wasn't afraid of anything. Fifteen years ago she cared about the blood and the boots and the bombs and she didn't care about yoga and her nails. Fifteen years ago she would have let go of that damn railing and she would have flown. And she wouldn't have even needed a happy thought.

She arrived home to hear the home theater, a.k.a. family room, booming. Kirk and the kids were watching a DVD that, she was sure, the little boy couldn't get her to let him watch.

When she poked her head around the corner they were enthralled with an action flick; the dinner dishes were precisely where she had seen them when she'd left. It was a comfort, almost, seeing them there, as if nothing had happened in her absence—as if nothing *could* happen in her absence to alter their world. She was the fulcrum, the mechanism by which all things rotated in order, and the pleasure it brought her warmed her in ways her sybaritic lifestyle pre-marriage had never been able to do.

As she viewed the scene, her notebook slipped from her hand, and in a rare moment of quiet, slapped against the floor.

The chorus of "hellos" came instantly with Kirk's benign interest in her "poetry adventure." Before she could answer, the booming started up again.

*It was fine.*

Her five-year-old son, the baby, circled around the couch and clasped his arms around her legs.

"Hi, my angel."

"Hi Mommy, Daddy said I could watch it and you went to your meeting but how come I have to go to bed at eight?"

"Go get in your pajamas, Sweetie."

His noises of protest reminded her of Hector on stage and she almost giggled, but a gurgle of emotion crept up instead. She mounted the stairs and caught a glimpse of the laundry baskets piled in the hallway, all ready to be dragged into the laundry room because tomorrow was laundry day. And casserole day. And t-ball at eleven.

An unwanted vision of Jade, reading, flowing, flowering, and Holly's throat gave way to a sob, sudden and harsh. *Polly Pan would laugh at me. Polly Pan would call me a chicken shit.* Holly stood with her back against the wall in the hallway. She slid down to her ass and her knees folded in close to her body. With her forehead resting against her knees, she wept with the bitter resentment she harbored only for herself. Jade would never sit that way, she was sure. And if she did, she'd write about it and it would be made into art.

Holly jumped at the site of little footie pajama feet standing in front of her. Her son's face looked untroubled.

"Why are you crying Mommy? Are you sad?"

"Yes, Mommy is sad."

She didn't believe in lying about her emotions to her kids because protecting them only postponed the inevitable, and the only inevitable was loss.

"Why are you so sad?"

"Because I grew up. That's why I'm sad."

"I growed up, too, Mommy."

"I don't want you to ever grow up, you hear me? You always stay this way. I lost myself, do you understand?"

He shook his head.

"These are not real!" She held up her hand, her French manicured nails in front of his face. "This is not who I am!" She yanked on her cream sweater, her taupe skirt. "Every day it's just me, Polly Pan, and *dirty clothes!*"

Her son shrunk back a little, his face puzzled.

"I used to have fabulous boots, you know? I used to have hats! I *smoked!*"

"Smoking is bad for you—"

"I didn't care because I would never grow old!"

Her hands covered her face, as if the tears themselves were obscene and not her words.

"And you know what I do all day?" She sobbed. "I do laundry! And I clean up and I schedule and I have errands! *My mother ran errands!*"

"What are errands?" he asked.

"Nothing…errands are *nothing*, Baby. Don't you see? Errands are napkins and smoke and mirrors and—and *bullshit!*"

His chin moved down to his chest and his eyes grew wide. He wasn't allowed to say *shit*. He stared at her and then, in a small voice:

"Errands are bullshit."

"Yes, they are bullshit." She looked at him, a red hue creeping into his cheeks.

Holding her gaze, his face crinkled into a toothy grin. He repeated the forbidden word. She took in deep breaths, tears still fresh.

He leaned over and wrapped his wiry limbs around her body. She unfolded her legs from their cocoon and held him, the sweet odor of his laundered pajamas and hair making her dizzy with love. When he finally released her he moved toward the stairs. He turned without a flicker of amusement on his face.

"So why are you sad, Mommy?"

She sighed. "Because, Angel, sometimes Mommies just get sad."

With that he smiled and hurried on his way.

# The Prayer

With all the chitter-chatter going on in her head, Ellen can't bear the television's ruckus a moment longer. Her seventeen-year-old, their baby, is spread over the couch like a weed patch. He can't ever share a space, and she files this fact away with the many others she has.

She stands in the doorway, knowing her face is sour, knowing that just her face sends him into a rage. Although her son is full of sound and fury, his father bellows louder; then Benjamin is reduced to his proper place with a bowed head and a "yes sir," and so she allows him to see her suffering.

"*What*?" He acknowledges her with his typical annoyance and she shakes her head, but tears form in the undersides of her lids.

"You go on outside now. You go on. You've been at it all day and you don't see the sun."

"I *see* the sun every friggin' day at school when I do *track*, Ma."

"Go on! And shut that beast off."

When Benjamin doesn't move, she walks over to the ancient set and slaps the knob in.

"Ma, why?"

"I just heard from your brother, Daniel, now, and he—" her voice cracks and Benjamin surrenders.

"Okay, okay, *jeez*, I'll go to Nathan's house. Can I use the car, at least?"

"He lives a block and a half away, Benjamin. You can use the legs God gave ya!"

This room is the den, and the desk has not seen light since her husband, Milt, had retired. There are papers upon envelopes upon printouts upon scads and scores of inspirational quotes lined up next to ancient paper weights. Lately he'd been cutting out the obituaries of friends and people he'd known, or even heard of, throughout his life. In the dark-wood-paneled basement room, the light only enters at the top window, and she can't see the fascination with her men and this room. While Milt spends hours at his desk, his absence in the afternoons leads Benjamin to inevitably haunt the room with his infernal television noise.

The magazine stacks in the holders have overgrown, and because she doesn't believe in waste, Ellen tidies up the stack as best she can, and moves the cardboard box of older periodicals closer to Milt's desk. She intermittently checks the stack, because her friends have told her boys hide things in the strangest places and she will not have that kind of thing in her home.

The television's silence causes her to turn around and look behind her, but all she sees is the illuminated staircase, the late afternoon sun shining light down into the dusky realm under her house. The den is the only finished room downstairs. The rest of it has a concrete floor that is only a giant slanting drain for the washer, dryer, and laundry tub in the corner.

She sits on her couch, the soft velvet a comfort, even though Benjamin, ever ungrateful, pokes fun at the wagon-wheels and orange-and-brown scheme. It's a couch-bed; it's useful. That boy can't understand "useful," and now, after speaking to Daniel, she sees her mistakes in bold color, underscored and highlighted. She sees she was soft, and had she made them do the right things more often, they would have been right.

"Damn him." She curses and walks to the edge of the room, where Benjamin had taken down the wooden cross she'd bought in Guatemala. It was hand-carved and the brown was slightly lighter than the wood paneling, so it showed up nicely. She searches around the floor, but finally locates it in Milt's bottom desk drawer.

She replaces it on the wall and reminds herself to file this away for the future. At once she wants to keep the boy home until he learns, but part of her believes he's already lost.

Like Daniel is now. *Daniel.*

*He's a good boy. He's a good, good boy.*

Her eyes fill with tears and she startles herself with an unexpected whimper.

Daniel had been courting Melinda for two-and-a-half years. That is an investment for a woman, aged thirty, especially one like Melinda. Ellen knows it wouldn't do to call and console Melinda because that isn't her place.

She had christened Melinda a mouse at first, knowing her handsome son could do better, but Melinda had stuck by Daniel, had been loyal and patient, and she deserves better than what Daniel has done to her.

Daniel said he'd be over tonight. He needed to talk to her and Milt, and at thirty-two years old, what could her son say to her and his father that he can't say over the phone?

The light on the stairs has dimmed and she wonders where Milt's gone to. She strains to hear their phone, but she can't hear it from down in the den. Milt turns off the ringer occasionally, which drives her crazy, because then how will she ever hear from anybody?

Ellen takes a look over the room as she stands to leave and reaches over to the side table where a collection of glasses has amassed. Holding them by their rims, she mounts the stairs and with each step up, her heart surges more and more painfully in her chest.

*Why in person? Why tonight?*

She'd invited Daniel and Melinda to dinner tonight, but Daniel told her they had parted ways last night. He wouldn't say why. Ellen is convinced her son would never have sullied Melinda and then released her. He had assured her only last month he had never touched Melinda overtly, and in *that way* and she believed him because he was a good, good boy.

The crock pot simmers on the counter and she flips the switch to *low* and crosses the room to the telephone. She picks it up and as a habit, puts it to her ear. She remembers then that it must be turned on. She turns it on, but can't remember where the ringer switch is. She dials her dearest friend's number and stands still, as if the phone still had a curly-cue cord attached to the wall unit.

"Hallo?" Beatrice's voice comforts her instantly, and she sighs.

"Bea, hello. Are you available to visit for a moment?"

"I am, yes. How is Milt?"

"Oh, he's out running the errands, you know. Your Kenneth all right?"

"Yes, he's fine. Out back with the bees. He's worried some neighbors went ahead with insecticide anyways and that's why they're droppin'."

"Oh dear, I'm sorry to hear."

"We'll see. How's the boys?"

Ellen and Bea speak three times a week, and the litany of familial complaints doesn't start until the small-talk and general goings-on are dismantled and brushed out of the way.

"That boy Benjamin, he's really a worry to me. I blame the TV. I blame the friends, but how do you fight those things?"

"I'm just glad we didn't have no stragglers. And I'm glad Missy's married off and good."

"I wish I could say it about Daniel."

"Well he's got that nice gal—"

"Not now, he doesn't."

"Oh, Ellen."

"I didn't see it coming. I can't believe it. Poor girl."

"Well did he break it off?"

"I don't know, he didn't say."

"Well then maybe she did."

This is a whole new perception for Ellen and her forehead aches from the depth of its contortion.

"I—she was a devoted little girl, Bea. Why just last week—"

"She's been devoted for what, three years?"

"Not quite three, no, but—"

51

"Maybe she was steppin' out on him. Found someone who'll commit to her. You know about girls when they get the itch for babies."

The mention of the grandchildren she would not enjoy for years to come rakes in Ellen's gut and she slumps into the plastic-covered chair in the kitchen and sighs. "Maybe that's why he's coming over tonight? To break it to us."

"You could find out easy enough."

"How? Call her mother?"

"No, Ellen, would she tell her mother a thing like that?"

"Well, no…"

"Okay then. You heard of the Facebook?"

"I heard. No idea about it…Benjamin talks and the like."

"You need to look on the Facebook. It's how my Annabelle keeps track of her daughters and friends and what not."

"Milt's gone and I can't get his computer up and going anyway."

"Doesn't your boy have that laptop he bought?"

"Well yes, it's in his room—"

"You go on that. You find that site and get an account."

"Oh Bea, I don't do with computers—"

"You remember how I'd set you up with the email?"

"Yes, I do. I forget to look at it, though."

"You remember it, though, dontcha?"

"I remember."

"You go up and you make a Facebook for yourself. You can see what happened because the kids, they tell everyone on it about everything. Get a pencil and paper, now, and I'll tell you step by step how you get it done."

Ellen hangs up with Bea, but after the instructions and after Bea tells her about Missy's new husband's sales job in Des Moines and how she wants to have a baby before their third wedding anniversary, Ellen can barely swallow for her envy. Bea already has two grandbabies. Now, with Melinda gone, who knows when Daniel would ever settle down?

Ellen stirs her stew and replaces the lid, the steam fogging her glasses for a moment. Clutching her instructions, she passes through the swinging doors out of the kitchen and walks up the short flight of stairs to Benjamin's room.

Out of habit she knocks—something she's wont to do, even though her husband tells her it's better to just walk in and surprise the boy.

The odor in the room is foreign, spoilt. She almost deciphers the smell of his sneakers amid the fetor of fried food and rank body stink. Benjamin forbids her to clean his room anymore, and now she knows this is just another mistake, another way she's soft and another way he isn't right.

Seeing his laptop on his unmade tumble of sheets and blankets, she kneels down on the floor next to his bed and pulls the computer toward her. It hums to life. Her hands hover over the keyboard as if she is offering them a blessing.

Up in the tabs she sees that Benjamin has the Facebook site already on. She takes a trembling finger and places it on the small, slightly rough square that Milt told her was the "mouse." A small arrow skates in sharp movements across the screen and when she sees it on the Facebook tab, she waits. When nothing happens, she taps the rectangle hesitantly and then the screen changes. So many names, so many pictures, she has no idea where to start.

She knows she's snooping but she reasons it's for her children's own good and she's always believed their protection is more important than their privacy. That's why they'd taken Daniel's door off the hinges when he was fifteen.

After looking at all of the names and not seeing Daniel's, Ellen traces the small arrow to the "search" box, and with two shaky fingers (even though she is a very proficient typist), she types in Daniel's name.

His page appears with a photo of his head, cropped from last year's males-only fishing trip with Milt and Benjamin. Daniel—her good boy. His tanned features and blue eyes bring a smile to her face instantaneously. She tricks herself into believing she hears someone behind her, and the blood rushes to her head as if Milt is standing right there, condemning her.

The small arrow moves easier, more confidently, as she peruses her son's page for any sign, any indication…

Down the page she sees Melinda's name. She skips the arrow down and tentatively pops it on the link to her name.

Her hand hangs in the air over the keyboard and her eyes adjust, but what she sees isn't what she allows herself to see. She reads the name again, she regards the picture again. *Yes, this was Melinda's page with her son's name on it.* The top of the page holds her eyes, the words a strangulating force on her neck. Finally she smoothes out the now-crumpled instructions Bea had given her.

Working on automatic, she creates an account (after several frustrating moments of trying to *remember* a password, not realizing she had to *create* one.) As if she'd been kicked in the chest, her breath ekes out in painful gasps, her hands tremble.

*What's on your mind?*

Her empty page asks her and she complies. With fingers more deft and succinct, she writes what's on her mind for the world to see.

She closes her eyes and rocks back and forth, hands in supplication, the words emblazoned on her page, asking for help, asking for forgiveness, wondering how her son had been so wronged by this woman for her to spread such lies about him. Such lies, for all to see.

He would come over tonight and he would tell his mother the truth, he would tell them that he wasn't the perv—the thing Melinda said. He would come to tell them he is still their good, good boy.

# Jesus Saves

**C**ulpability comes in many colors, but none as stark as the color red. So she avoided that color, avoided wearing it like vile odor. It was one of the many ways she was good. The one exception was, of course, the cashmere sweater she wore to Christmas services, the sweater she had saved for and bought that made Mama's face pucker. Kerasel couldn't recall her mother ever wearing red.

Kerasel ran her hand in a light, hovering caress over the tops of her cashmere wool sweaters and closed her eyes. Fingering each one, she delighted in the uniformity, the flocculent tickle of the knit on her skin…she recoiled and pulled her hand out of the folds. Sensual pleasure was one of the ways she was bad. She stepped away and smoothed her skirt, hating the aching fullness that touching her sweaters provoked.

Her mother called her down, because her breakfast awaited her and the bus would *not* wait for her, so she chose her baby-pink cashmere with the tiny pearl buttons. She slipped it on over her blouse that covered her new satin-like camisole that covered her underthings. She'd also bought the camisole with money from her savings, had worked hard all summer babysitting. Her mother wouldn't buy it.

"This white one's more practical. And look, it's five dollars cheaper," she said, scowling at her daughter.

"But I like this *beige* one."

Her mother moved close to her then and pinched her upper arm, right there in Marshall's.

"*I know why you like it.* I know why young girls like such things and don't you tell me I don't!"

"No, Mama, it won't show through—"

"You like the fabric, don't you tell me you don't! It's shameful, that feeling, *don't you forget that.*"

Kerasel defied her mother and bought it anyway, telling her the beige color was to ensure she would be modest when she wore shirts, as the spring days would be too warm for sweaters. But the camisole was new and lustrous and grazed her belly with cool strokes. When she wore it the first time, her lower body warmed with that uncomfortable fullness that dissolved into a tacky mess. She had to clean up in the restroom, her face the color of her Christmas sweater.

She fastened each pearl button and played a game of trying to wait to touch the wool, trying to avoid its downy feel as she eased the buttons through their tiny slits.

The morning was crisp and her breath puffed out in a haze in front of her face. Looking down on the porch, she saw that another flyer had been slipped under their rough welcome mat. The paper was heavy and damp with chilly dew. The flyer wasn't from their congregation, but it promised relief from spiritual pain. She'd seen ads like it before; Mama said they were for sinners. It promised salvation and the phone number was in bold black letters. She left it there, knowing her mother would not want her to touch it, knowing her mother would crumple it up and throw it away.

Hoarfrost clung to the sallow and depleted grasses and the rimy dirt showed through. Their front yard never seemed to green anymore. Since Daddy died, the grass grew wild and unkempt, the bushes spread voluptuous and full. As soon as the days grew hot, the sun scorched the grass and ground, leaving them charred and arid.

Kerasel looked back at the dingy picture window and saw her mother, face hovering like an apparition. Mama's instant smile was tight, an eraser effacing whatever emotion had been gracing it before. Kerasel brought her hand up and her fingers twiddled in the air. Her mother nodded her head, eyes piercing, and disappeared. Mama saw her off every day, had seen her off every day, even the day her father died a year and a half ago. Even on that day, Mama still said goodbye.

The grumble of the bus could be heard long before it arrived, and Kerasel pulled her books closer to her chest to quell the nervous ache inside her. Every day the ache dogged her, hungry and angry and scarlet as sin. Some days before class she had to visit the restroom to clean up, the moisture scaring her, the scent alarming her, and she fretted that everyone would know. The days she wore the camisole were worse and she knew Mama was right—wanting the beige one was bad.

Her biggest challenge, the one she prayed over every night, was in her last class period, history class. Jarvis Pitts called her his "Little Lamb" on account of her last name being Lamb. The familiarity warmed her, warned her, and on days when she was good, she asked Jesus to protect her from that warmth. But some days when she was bad she didn't talk to Jesus because she didn't want Him to see her writing notes in response to Jarvis's rough jottings he passed to her from behind.

Sometimes he only drew pictures and they made no sense to her at all. Once in a while they did make sense and on those days she rewarded his artistic efforts with opprobrium followed by a prayer to Jesus because the cashmere on her arms was so soft under her touch, and her insides seemed to burst from being so full. Other times she'd write him back with scripture or hymns; he'd turn them dirty and she would rededicate herself to Mrs. Horne's lecture. At those times she could almost shut his rough features out altogether.

He used a red pencil to draw things and say things that caused her stomach to flutter and things lower to swell in *that way*. If she saw him in the hall he'd waggle his tongue at her like a serpent, and she hated the way her face heated and blushed.

Jarvis was a year older but he was held back after seventh grade. Since then he haunted her in at least one class each year. A loud and raucous boy, he saved his most evil taunts for her and she loathed him. She also knew on some level he needed her. He didn't have a mama, didn't know any better. She couldn't be outright cruel. Throughout the years as he grew, he broadened in his shoulders, his wavy blond hair fell into his eyes, and the way he looked at her ruptured her poise and caused her to perspire and shift in her skin. He just needed a mother to help him see, help him know how to be good.

The day had dragged on, and when the last bell rang Kerasel saw his stare in the hall, his smile, and she chose that moment to become conscious of the camisole rubbing against her belly. Afraid she'd started her woman's time, she rushed to the bathroom only to find she was not bleeding at all, but messy and sticky nonetheless and with quaking hands she pulled out reams of toilet paper to erase it. She washed her hands, applied some balm to her lips (Mama disapproved of shiny lips, too), and hurried out into the already desolate hall. Her harried pace to the outer doors was futile, as she couldn't even hear the bus' engine any longer.

Mama was at work and couldn't come pick her up. Dreading the long walk as the afternoon sun beat on her back, she headed for home.

There weren't many cars at this time of day. The small community that housed the high school and middle school seemed vacant, abandoned, as if she were already home, already in the middle of nowhere. Each pebble poked through her Mary Jane's as she tramped toward the main highway that would eventually lead to her isolated house.

When she heard a car slowing behind her, she kept her eyes forward. A honk caused her to make a small *yip* sound, and she veered to the grass-and-pebbled shoulder and spun around.

Jarvis Pitts leaned over the seat in his ancient pickup, the red and white colors muted by rust and peeling paint. His arm was casually over the back of the seat and he smiled, as if her discomposure delighted him.

"Why you walkin'?"

"Because I *want* to walk." Kerasel turned on her heel and reminded herself of the house rule that she isn't to get into cars with boys alone, ever, no matter what. But her feet were hurting and a glimmer of hope appeared as she steeled herself for another honk. When he tapped the horn again, she whirled around scowling.

"I am not some herd of *sheep*, Jarvis. Stop honking at me!"

The disingenuous downturn of his mouth caused her to *hrumph* in disgust.

"Listen, I'll give ya a lift. C'mon now, don't be like that. Look, see?" He gunned his engine and pulled the truck a few feet ahead of her on the shoulder. He jumped out of the driver's side, and while wiping his hands on his pants, he walked 'round to the passenger's side and opened the door with a sweeping motion of his arm.

"All gentleman-like. See?" He smiled and for an instant, his teeth gleamed, and the deepening of the dimple in his cheek caused warmth to trickle down in her gut.

She stood staring at him and considered the long walk home. Looking around the road and houses, she approached warily.

"Miss Lamb, I would like to please take you home. Alright? I gotta go to work, anyways, so I'm headin' that way."

"You don't work by my house," she said, scowling.

"Well I know, but I drive right by your road."

"How do you know where I live, anyway?"

"I just know your road. I used to take the bus, 'member?"

She edged near the pickup, keeping her distance, because how could anyone think her a good person if she got into that truck?

"Just this once 'cause I have a lot of homework."

Moving quick and almost touching the dirty truck panel, she moved past him, grabbing hold of the armrest on the door to get inside. The handle broke off on one side as she slid in.

"Oh, I-I'm sorry." She looked at him and he grinned.

"Been broke since I got it. You didn't do nothin' to it."

He raced around the back, got in next to her, and gunned the engine again, not bothering to look behind him. Her arms flailed out as she sought a place to steady herself. She placed her books next to her on the seat, a wall he could not penetrate with his rough hands and stringy hair.

"You drive yet?" he asked.

"I take driver's courses next fall."

"Still a baby, then." He chuckled and her jaw stiffened.

"I'm not a baby."

"Oh yeah? Prove it." He raised one eyebrow and she swallowed thickly and turned away from him. The wind tousled her hair and her tresses kept sticking to her lips. She pulled her locks in back of her and caught him staring at her.

"Staring's rude."

"I like starin'. Anyways it's a compliment."

She picked her books back up and held them to her chest as the truck approached the turn-off. The road up to her house was unpaved, and a familiar flush crept up her cheeks as she steeled herself. "You can drop me off here, where the bus does."

"I can just drive you up. Look, I got a truck. It can go on bumpy roads."

The truck bumped along, jarring her as she watched her house come into full view down the lane. She couldn't take her eyes off of the once-white lattice porch, now gray, defiled and peeling. She wished the overgrowth of bushes came high enough to conceal its disgrace. There was no garage, just trees lining either side of the place, the dead grass in the fields somehow giving off perfume in the warm, humid air.

She pointed silently.

"This it?" he asked.

"Yes, this is it."

He pulled in front and whipped the truck around so she was closer to the walkway.

"It's old." He peered at her house as if it was a specimen of insect he'd never seen.

"It's an *antique*." She shot back, clutching her books to her.

He laughed out loud then. "Houses ain't *antique*."

She ignored him. Opening the creaking door, she slid off the slick seat. "Thank you for the ride."

His door slammed as she strode to her front door, his feet crunching on the grass behind her. The other house rule loomed in her mind.

"What are you doing?" she asked, pivoting.

60

"I gotta drive another twenty miles and I was wonderin' if I could have a drink of water and maybe use...you know...your..."

"I'm not allowed to have anyone in the house." She instantly regretted her revelation and looked down. She saw her mother hadn't disposed of the ad under the mat, and she sought another explanation, pulling the now-dried flyer farther out with her toe. "What I mean is, someone'll be home any minute."

"I gave you a *ride*! And anyways, I'm gonna be late for work, but I'm *dyin'*. Please? For just a second is all."

She didn't want to think of the business he had in her bathroom because it was too intimate to imagine him doing that in her home with no one there. But the thoughts whittled away at her resolve and her breath became shallow. When she met his gaze, his eyes were open wide. She looked up the road and then back at him.

"Fine. But you don't tell anyone 'bout this. Just come in. For a *second*."

"Thank you, Miss Lamb."

"You don't have to call me that."

He stopped in front of her, altogether too close; she had no way to back up. "I *like* callin' you that."

Her face turned away from him, but her heart palpitated clear through to her soft sweater, now so uncomfortably confining that she wanted to flap her arms at the elbows just to get some air.

His presence in the house was feral, and she regretted having taken pity on him, but it was too late. Past the family photos hanging on the wall she walked, with him too close behind her. She walked past the bathroom and pointed into the dark. Then:

"It's in there."

He tipped his head to her and laughed again as she purled in a circle away from him.

As the bathroom door closed, she hurried to her bedroom to check her appearance. Seeing her disheveled hair and pale face in her dresser mirror, she grabbed her brush.

Overlooking her bed was a picture of Jesus her aunt had given her on her baptism day. Too ashamed to communicate with Him like she normally would, she looked away and at her reflection. Wide eyes stared back at her in the dusky mirror.

*My furniture is antique*, she fumed.

Dragging her brush through her hair, she searched her dresser top for some lip balm. Not finding any handy, she turned and jumped at the sight of Jarvis in her open doorway.

"You can't come in here."

"'Zis your room?"

"You can't be *in* here, Jarvis…"

Arms folded, her hands rubbed her sweater, and she walked toward him but he blocked the door. "Why not?" he said, eyes smiling.

She tried to move past him but he caught her up in his arms and kissed her. Volts of energy passed through her, and she couldn't will her body to twist free of him. Only when his kisses deepened did she come to life and try to push him back.

"Stop it—you need to get *out*—"

"Hush now, come on." He grabbed her around her waist and pulled her to her single bed, made with a single pink pillow on its creamy white coverlet. She tried to get up but he was on her, his body spanning the length of hers and she moved to get free. The decorum from earlier that afternoon somehow remained with her, and so her attempts were timid—polite even.

"Jarvis, *please…*"

When she turned her cheek to him, he brought her face forward with a strong clasp around her chin. He kissed her and his hand move between them, below her belly button. Her legs panicked before she could articulate a protest.

"Hold still, shh…"

"No! What are you—?"

She squirmed and his body got heavier. She inhaled with a sharp gasp as he lifted up only slightly and she saw a foreign thing, like nothing she'd ever seen. She didn't want to see any more. She squeezed her eyes shut and whimpered, struggling mightily now. She rotated her hips but that only seemed to scrunch her skirt up farther on her legs.

"Hush now." His voice was strangled and his hand bruised her forearm as his other hand worked in between their bodies.

"Get offa me, Jarvis!"

Jarvis moved his hand from in between them and grasped the top of her sweater. With a violent jerk of his arm, it flew open, the tiny pearl buttons clitter-clattering against her antique dresser. The noise arrested her and she stopped moving, but her body was stiff as cold steel.

A hard pressure on her pubic bone brought her out of her daze, and as she wriggled, his forearm moved across her neck.

She tried to cough but it caught. The noise coming from her was a high-pitched moan, but he did things between their bodies she couldn't feel, as if he'd given up on her skirt and only worked the mysterious region near his pants.

Hot flesh seared her inner thigh and although she knew about men and women, she had never before worked out the particulars, never imagined the force, the frenzy with which it could happen.

His hand moved up to her shirt and as he shoved rough fingers inside, the thought flashed through her mind that he would feel the silky camisole, feel her sin, and think she wanted this from him. The picture of Jesus hung above her head, silently suffering, gazing away from her. She stared at His averted eyes and silently prayed with everything in her for Him to help her, forgive her, please, please, help. She promised Him that she would always be good, never be bad, from now on.

Jarvis jerked his body on her and she emitted helpless gasps, writhing to be free. Finally he rose up from her with an agonized groan. Her breath heaved out and she could barely inhale. Warm moisture scalded her upper leg and underpants and she felt it oozing down her inner thigh. Her throat convulsed in agitated attempts to swallow, but it seemed to be stuck, like a clogged pump. Jarvis rolled off of her and stood on the floor next to the bed. He did up his pants and then turned to her and held out his hand for hers. The moisture turned icy under her skirt.

Her lips were sealed shut and her limbs would not obey, so he grabbed her rigid hand from off of her coverlet and pulled her to standing. She stumbled toward him and he caught her. In a peculiar moment, reminiscent of the eons of time that had passed since he opened the truck door for her, he kissed the top of her head. Pulling her behind him, he led her down the hall, her legs quaking and numb, the sticky stuff tickling her maddeningly as she stumbled along.

He opened the front door and turned, his expression uncalculating.

"Don't worry 'bout the water. See ya tomorrow." Without looking at her again, he bounded down the porch stairs and sauntered to his truck. He waved to her once while inside the cab, and her arm, feeling disembodied, rose to return the gesture. Aware of the moisture trickling down the back of her knee, she squeezed her still-convulsing thighs together and glanced down, expecting to see evidence of Jarvis and his now-inconceivable presence.

The ad under the mat flapped in the late afternoon gusts as loose dirt scurried past her shoes on the ashen porch. She pulled the ad free and walked into the house, shutting the door quietly behind her.

In the bedside drawer of her mother's room, she found the bottle of pills Mama had been given after Daddy died. Mama kept them *just in case*, but she never did have insomnia again. The pills came up a third of the way in the bottle, which was plenty.

Kerasel moved into the kitchen, breathing through her mouth, terrified she would smell him on her, smell his presence in the house. In the cupboard next to the sink she pulled down a glass, water spots covering the rim, and filled it, eerily redolent of her plans only moments ago, plans to give Jarvis a drink, plans to get him in and out of the house quickly and thank him and be good.

The pills were ghostly white on the table, and she counted thirteen. Thirteen was when she first bled, and it seemed like an inspiration, an answer to her prayer.

The flyer lay stiff and smudged on the table, and she reached over to the small telephone stand next to her chair and dialed the number written in bold lettering.

The ringing sounded so far away, and so did the chipper voice that answered.

"Jesus Saves, this is Betty!"

Kerasel took in a shuddering breath, and her voice, as if through sandpaper, eked out.

"Hello?"

# A White House

One nation under him, one Commander-in-chief under *Him*. Things tend to make sense here, in the opulent silence of the all-white room. Privileged silence. He pushes back the vision of the impoverished multitudes huddled together in this lavish chamber, dirty-faced Olivers holding up their dishes for more. It helps if he envisions them all in white.

The Mormon temple is closed to the public today just for him. Security won't allow him to attend with other Saints. Yet communion with his Father in Heaven feels vacant rather than intimate today. When others have milled about him in the utter stillness, his conviction seems to meld with theirs, becoming alive and strong, a thriving child with lungs full of air.

His cabinet awaits him back in his office, ready to tell him how to proceed. He had been ashamed to tell them he needs this parley. This isn't, then, about the re-election. It's about what's right. The right thing isn't to air-lift people from the streets and bring them here for the excellent food, each of the hundreds of altar rooms replaced with a bed. Allowing his mind to assess the feasibility of this fantasy is something he won't do.

How he shrinks from his own mind. How his thoughts displease God, he can feel that, the utter solitude of the wrong-ness of his contemplation. With God, there's an established order, just as with the world. No one can airlift the broken, hopeless, the weary. They must lift themselves. This thought feels at last in concert with God. Tears fill his eyes because he remembers the feeling of being in accord with God. It comes with right thinking, it comes with preserving order.

When he's surrounded by the pragmatists, concerned with campaigns, concerned with pleasing people who put him in that office, the voice of his Father is silent. When he'd been elected, he thought every signature would feel a loving hand guiding it. Instead, his hand feels interminably alone. He simply has to find the *reason*. He knows, however, that reason is the enemy to the Holy Spirit guiding him. This is why the peace has been shattered today, why amity in this sumptuous room deserts him again and again. He must not think—he must only feel.

The hard medicine. His Father in Heaven allows his children the hard medicine in order for them to grow, yet he had not counted on being the cup from which the people would drink. *Ask and ye shall receive.* He asks, he asks, he knocks. Never before has he been faced with answers that all seem wrong. One more cut, says his Vice President, one more cut and we'll be on track.

But the cut runs deep, down his chest, down to his gut where the masses lie in wait, beseeching him. They had questioned electing a Latter-Day Saint. He quashed his religion for the sake of the polls, and now he wonders if he didn't quash the very fiber that telegraphed his Father's presence in him. But no, he had felt it, hadn't he? Just now?

He's not ashamed. How many presidents have fallen to their knees when they knew not what they should do? He is no different. Yet he is different in that he has the one and only Truth. He had prayed for guidance on how to choose his advisors. But he is the man here, in this room, communing with God. The others are just men. His is a silence they will never know. He is chosen. *Thy will be done.*

JA Carter-Winward lives and writes in the mountains
of northern Utah.

**Other works by the author:**

*Always Listen to the Ravings of a Mad Woman* **(under Henneman)**

*TDTM*

*Falling Back to Earth*

*no apologies* **(poetry)**

*The Rub*

**Coming Soon:** *Grind*